FLAT STANLEY

Plays Ball

EGMONT

We bring stories to life

Book Band: Green

First published in Great Britain 2013
by Egmont UK Ltd
The Yellow Building, 1 Nicholas Road, London W11 4AN

Text and illustrations copyright © 2013 by the Trust u/w/o Richard C. Brown
a/k/a Jeff Brown f/b/o Duncan Brown
Illustrations by Jon Mitchell

ISBN 978 1 4052 5955 2

10 9 8 7 6 5 4 3 2 1

A CIP catalogue record for this title is available from the British Library.

Printed in Singapore.

47001/1

FLAT STANLEY
Plays Ball

Written by **Lori Haskins Houran**   Illustrations by **Jon Mitchell**

Based on the original character created by **Jeff Brown**

Blue Bananas

Stanley Lambchop lived with his mother, his father, and his little brother, Arthur.

Stanley was four feet tall,
about a foot wide,
and half an inch thick.

He had been flat ever since
a bulletin board fell on him.

Sometimes being flat
was a bit tricky.

When he turned sideways,
Stanley was hard to spot.

And a big gust of wind
could sweep Stanley off his feet.

But he never let his flatness get in his way.

'I'm trying out for the rounders team,' Stanley told Arthur one day.

Arthur helped Stanley practise.

Stanley hit a thousand balls.

He caught a thousand catches.

Stanley's hard work was rewarded.

'Congratulations,' said Coach Bart.

'You're on the team!'

Sports day was bright and breezy.

The teams ran on to the field.

'There's Stanley!' cried Arthur.

Mr Lambchop snapped a picture.

Mrs Lambchop cheered.

'Hooray for the other players too,'

she added politely.

Stanley was the first batter.

He stepped up to the batting square,

turned sideways,

and pulled back his bat.

The bowler squinted at Stanley.

'This guy is so skinny,' he said,

'I can hardly see where to throw.'

He bowled a ball.

'No ball,' said the umpire.

The bowler bowled again.

'No ball,' repeated the umpire,
and Stanley ran to the first post.

'Good job!' called Coach Bart.

Stanley's team played well.

Soon they were winning.

The other team had one last chance.
Their best batter came in to bat,
and blasted the ball into the air!

Just then, the breeze picked up.

Stanley ran and leaped into the wind.

WHOOSH! Up floated Stanley.

PLUNK went the ball into his hand!

'Great catch!' Arthur cried.

Not everyone agreed.

'That's not fair,' yelled someone in the crowd.

'Are flat players even allowed?'

Stanley felt crushed.

That night, Stanley talked to Arthur.

'I'm a good player,' he said.

'And not just because I'm flat.

But how can I prove it?'

Arthur looked out the window.

Then he smiled.

'I think I know a way.'

The day of the second game
was bright and breezy again.
But something was different.
'Stanley!' gasped Mrs Lambchop.

Her son was not flat.

He was bursting out of his shirt!

Mrs Lambchop gasped again.

'My nice clean laundry!'

A sock stuck out of Stanley's collar.

A pink, frilly blouse trailed from the leg of his trousers.

'That's my favourite one!' she said.

There was no time to worry
about the clothes.
A batter smacked the ball
high into the air!

Stanley ran and leaped into the wind.
But this time Stanley didn't float up,
and the ball didn't land in his hand.
It sailed right over his head.

Soon it was Stanley's turn to bat.
The bowler had no trouble
seeing where to bowl now.

'Good ball,' called the umpire.

Stanley ran for the first post,

but the fielder was too quick.

Stanley was out!

In the crowd, Arthur gulped.
Had he made a terrible mistake
helping Stanley unflatten himself?

Soon the game was nearly over.

The score was tied.

Stanley came in to bat again.

He heard Arthur's voice in the crowd.

'Come on, Stanley! You can do it!'

The bowler bowled the ball . . .

and Stanley SMASHED it!

The ball flew miles.

But a fielder ran after it.

Meanwhile, Stanley tore

around the posts.

First post. Second post. Third post.

Stanley was headed for the fourth post!

But so was the ball!

'Stanley, SLIDE!' shouted Coach Bart.

Arthur's heart raced.

If Stanley were still flat, he could slide easily under the catcher's hand.

But now?

Stanley stretched out his arms
and dived.

There was a swirl of dirt and socks.

Then the umpire called, 'In!'

'Wahoo!' Arthur hollered.

Mr and Mrs Lambchop clapped
so hard their hands hurt.

'That's not fair,' yelled someone
in the crowd.

'Look at the muscles on that kid.
Are players that big even allowed?'
Stanley grinned.

'Not so many socks next time,'
Mr Lambchop called to Stanley.
Mrs Lambchop looked at Arthur.
'And NO blouses!'